Reading

Copyright © 1980, Raintree Publishers Inc.

All rights reserved. No part of this book may be reproduced or utilized in any form or by any means, electronic or mechanical, including photocopying, recording, or by any information storage and retrieval system, without permission in writing from the Publisher. Inquiries should be addressed to Raintree Childrens Books, 330 East Kilbourn Avenue, Milwaukee, Wisconsin 53202.

Library of Congress Number: 80-16547

5 6 7 8 9 89 88 87 86 85

Printed in the United States of America.

Library of Congress Cataloging in Publication Data

Allington, Richard L.
  Reading.

  (Beginning to learn about)
  SUMMARY: Situations taken from daily life demonstrate the usefulness and pleasure of reading.
  1.   Books and reading for children — Juvenile literature. [1.   Reading] I.   Krull, Kathleen, joint author.   II.   Naprstek, Joel.   III.   Title.
IV.   Series.
Z1037.A1A1027   028.5'5   80-16547

Richard L. Allington is Associate Professor, Department of Reading,
State University of New York at Albany.
Kathleen Krull is the author of nineteen books for children.

BEGINNING TO LEARN ABOUT

READING

BY RICHARD L. ALLINGTON, PH.D., · AND KATHLEEN KRULL
ILLUSTRATED BY JOEL NAPRSTEK

Raintree Childrens Books • Milwaukee • Toronto • Melbourne • London

Have you ever wondered why we read?
This story will show you some of the reasons:

for fun

to learn new things

to get around

to avoid danger

As you read this story, tell why we would
want to read the words in each picture.
Then read the story again. Tell what might
happen if we couldn't read the words.

Caution-
Do not use
near fire-
Harmful if
swallowed

On Saturday, I helped
my sister paint the fence.

Menu

Hamburger　　　**Pizza**

French Fries　　**Milk**

My sister took me to a
new restaurant for lunch.

Then we decided to go to a movie. First we picked out the one we wanted to see.

You are invited to the greatest party ever. Please call if you can't come.

When we got home, there was a letter waiting for me.

On Sunday, I went to the zoo
with my family.

We saw lions at the zoo.

We stopped at the ice-cream stand.

On the way home,
we bought a newspaper.

On Monday, I went to school.
I rode my bicycle.

At school, we each picked out
a book we wanted to read.

At lunchtime, I saw that many kids
had lunch boxes just like mine.

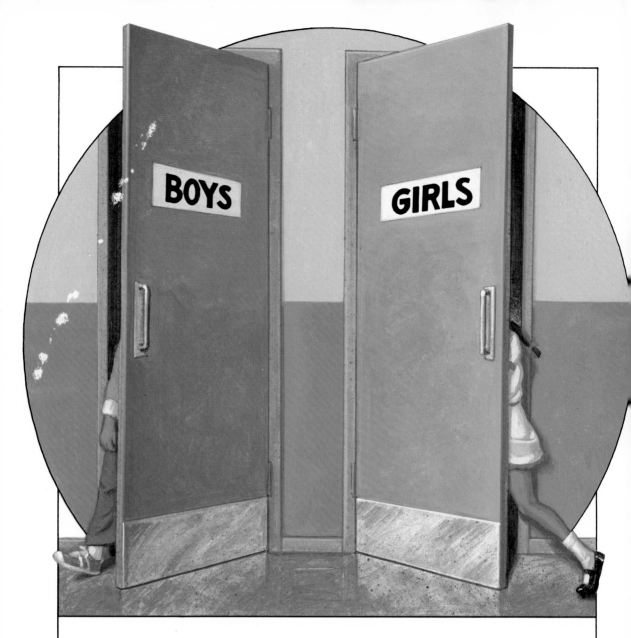

After lunch, I had to use
the bathroom.

On Tuesday, I went to the library
to find out more about the lions
at the zoo.

Rules of
the game

After school, I asked some of my
friends over to play a new game.

My best friend brought me
a beautiful present.

I made cookies for my friends.

On Wednesday it rained.
I took the bus to school.

After school, I went to the store to buy
a thank-you card for my best friend.

Then I decided to go to the toy store
to buy a present for my friend.

I had to take the elevator
to the right floor.

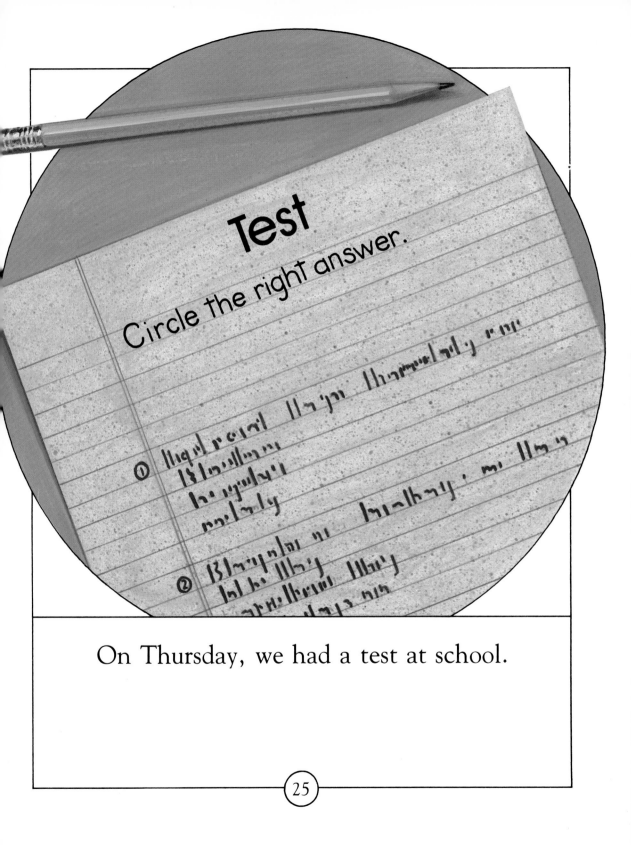

On Thursday, we had a test at school.

On the playground, we played
hide-and-seek.

On the way home from school,
I went to the store to buy milk.

After dinner, I wanted to watch
my favorite program on TV.

On Friday, my pet turtle got sick.

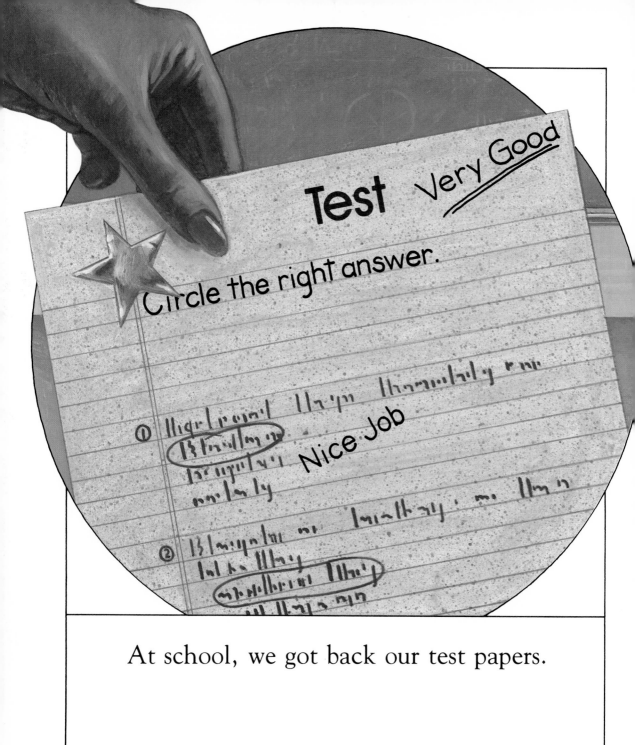

At school, we got back our test papers.

Later, I found a note on my desk
from a brand-new friend.
I was glad I knew how to read.

Take a walk around your neighborhood.
How many signs can you read?
You can look for signs that tell you

what street you are on
where to find something you want to buy
where the bus stops
where there is danger
what hours a store is open
where to eat
where the fire alarm is
where to get something fixed
where to mail a letter
where it is safe to cross the street

Tell what might happen if you couldn't read the signs.

Make your own book about reading.
Look at a newspaper or magazine.
Find pictures of people reading.
Cut out the pictures. Tape or
paste them onto pieces of paper.
Fasten the papers together.
Tell why each person is reading.
You may ask an adult to help you.